DAVID B and the TERRIBLE

To Rory -
I hope you enjoy the adventures of the David B!
- Christine

Written by Christine Smith and Illustrated by Rebecca Rothman
Old Heavy Duty Publishing

David B and the Terrible Rocks

Copyright © 2019 by Christine Smith and Illustrated by Rebecca Rothman
All rights reserved. No part of this book may be used or reproduced in any manner without the written permission of the publisher, except where permitted by law.

Publication Date: January, 2019

Price: $19.95 ISBN:13: 978-0-9890010-1-4

Library of Congress Control Number: 2018964214

Pages 44 | Illustrations 44 | Word Bank with Definitions Ages: 5-8

Publisher: Old Heavy Duty Publishing PO Box 1431 Bellingham, WA 98227
www.oldheavydutypublishing.northwestnavigation.com
sales@oldheavydutypublishing.northwestnavigation.com
info@oldheavydutypublishing.northwestnavigation.com

Subjects: Children | Boats | Nature | Animals | Pacific NW | Alaska | Salish Sea | Maritime

Book Description: David B didn't want to go home to Comfy Cove. He wanted to stay up late, just like the big boats that would pass by his anchorage in the middle of the night. Instead of going home, he decided to keep on exploring. As day turned to night, David B marveled at how the water sparkled in the moonlight. The moon began to set, and his wonder turned into caution then fear as he remembered an old tale of boat-eating rocks that would come to life on moonless nights. In the dark, he hears something breathing, but it's not the scary rocks. It's something else…

Author Christine Smith: Christine grew up in the Pacific Northwest. She is most at home in the space where the forests meet the ocean. Her favorite things are the earthy smells of a seaweed encrusted beach on a hot day and the excitement of discovery, whether it's learning how a bear digs for clams, or how a tree communicates with insects. Christine sees the world as filled with wonder. Her time on the real David B has helped her to bring that same sense of excitement and discovery to people both on and off the boat.
www.northwestnavigation.com

Illustrator Rebecca Rothman: Rececca is an illustrator and graphic designer living in Seattle. Growing up on a steady diet of Edward Gorey, Maurice Sendak and Beatrix Potter – she naturally found her happy place in the cozy space between spooky and quaint. She is inspired by the connection between all forms of life, and believes tiny acts of kindness can change the world.
www.rebecca-rothman.com

Deep in the heart of the Great Salmon Sea, there lived a young boat named David B, who loved to sing his CHUG-CHUG-CHUG song all day as he navigated up and down the narrow channels.

He'd sing **CHUG-CHUG-CHUG** to his friends Randall Raven, Sophie Seal, and Bella Bear.
He especially loved to sing to the wise old trees on shore.

One evening as the sun began to set, David B didn't want to stop. He didn't want to drop his anchor for the night. He didn't want to go to sleep. He just wanted to keep CHUG-CHUG-CHUGGING along.

He wondered what it would be like to navigate at night under a moonlit sky just like the big cruise ships and tugboats.

For hours David B sang CHUG-CHUG-CHUG.
The water sparkled in the moonlight.

Wherever he went, the moon seemed to follow.
He felt like the moon was his best friend.
He felt like he could navigate the narrow channels forever.

As the night wore on, the moon began to hang low in the sky.

He realized that soon, he'd be alone in the dark without his friend the moon. His voice began to waiver. He began to feel afraid.

Just before the moon set and all the light was gone, David B recalled an old tale. A tale where the rocks come to life on moonless nights.

They would come to life for a terrible feast.

A FEAST of BOATS!

DAVID B

He tried to forget about the tale of the terrible rocks.

He tried to sing CHUG-CHUG-CHUG, but he was too scared.

He couldn't think about anything else.

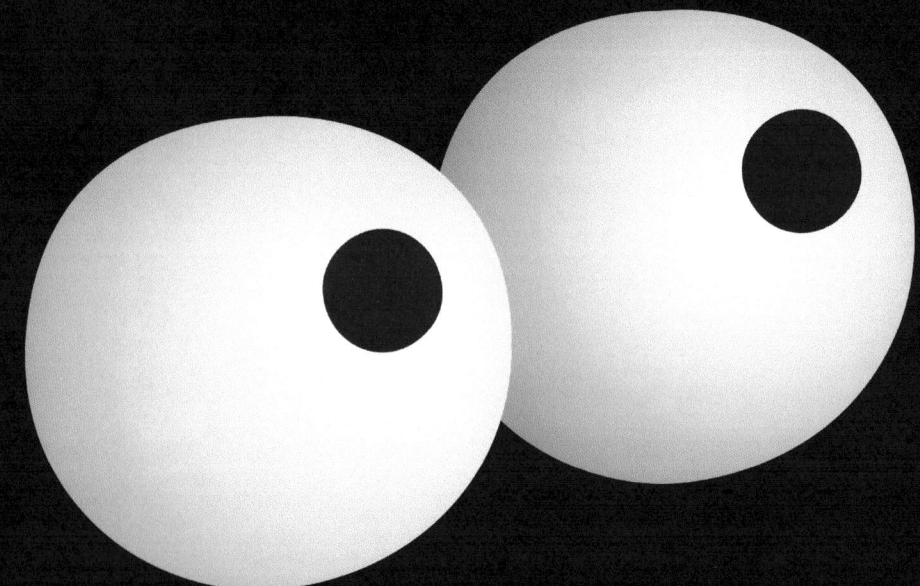

"THOSE ROCKS! THOSE TERRIBLE ROCKS!

What if they do come to life?

What if they do gather for a terrible feast? A FEAST OF BOATS!"

David B's timbers shivered.

Without his friend the moon the channel felt narrower.

The water seemed shallower,

and the rocks, those terrible rocks…

He knew they must be alive.

In the darkness he thought he heard something.

Even though it was too dark to see, David B looked left and he looked right.

He spun in a circle.

NOTHING WAS THERE.

David B trembled.

He felt like his engine was racing, but he was too afraid to move.

David B closed his eyes tight and revved up his engine as fast as it would go.
He sounded his horn and shouted at the top of his pipes …

INTO DAVID B STEW YOU TERRIBLE, LAUGHING, GIGGLING ROCKS!

He slowly opened his eyes.

Instead of terrible rocks and darkness, he was surprised to see the water shimmering with a million-gazillion teeny-tiny sparkling lights, and a pod of laughing, splashing, giggling porpoises.

One porpoise swam up to David B and said... "Hi, I'm Dolly! These are my friends, Thea, Oswell, Lindsey, and Garth. Are you ok?"

"Who are you, and what's with the terrible, giggling, laughing, boat-eating rocks?"

"I'm David B. I wanted to stay up all night long and sing CHUG-CHUG-CHUG in the moonlight. Then the moon went away, and I got scared. I was afraid the rocks would come to life and make me into stew for their moonless feast."

"David B – you are too funny! Rocks don't come to life and eat boats. You have nothing to be afraid of. The dark is when you can play in the sea sparkles."

"SEA SPARKLES? What are those?

I've never seen them before."

David B spun his propeller and made a big turn.
The water lit up with a beautiful blue-green glow.

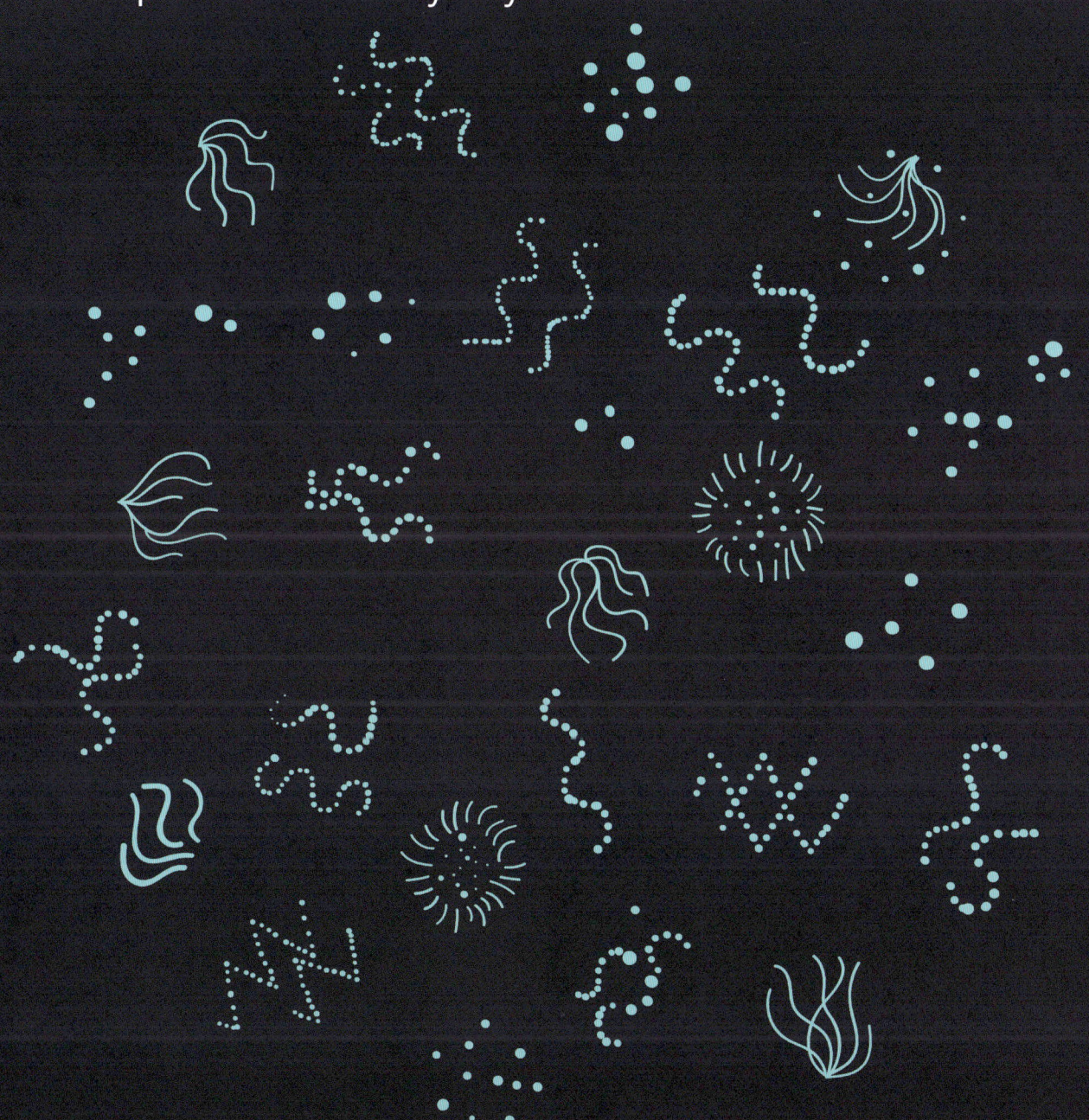

"Sea sparkles are teeny-tiny creatures that live in the ocean.

When you swirl them, they make their own light."

Dolly and the other porpoises gathered around David B's bow.

Dolly looked up at him, "Do you want to come play in the sea sparkles with us? We'd love to hear your CHUG-CHUG-CHUG song."

"**YES, I DO!** I want to play in the sea sparkles, too."

"Well come along, David B, let's hear you sing!" said Dolly.

David B powered up his engine and began to sing, **CHUG-CHUG-CHUG**. The porpoises followed close to him, surfacing, laughing, and giggling as the sea sparkles washed over them. David B forgot all about the terrible rocks.

All too soon the sun's rays began to reach for the sky.
The sea sparkles faded with the morning twilight.

"It's time for us to go", Dolly said.

"But, let's meet again.
 We'll have many more adventures exploring the Great Salmon Sea."

He was happy he learned how to navigate at night, just like the big boats ...

but he was happier still, that he made new friends.

Friends that he knew he'd see again.

DAVID B's WORLD

Where is the Great Salmon Sea?

The Great Salmon Sea is a make-believe place based on the many places where the real David B travels in the Pacific Northwest, Canada, and Alaska.

What kind of porpoise is Dolly?

Dolly and her friends are Dalls Porpoises. They love to eat small fish and are fast swimmers, swimming around 34 miles per hour. Dalls porpoises also enjoy playing on bows of moving boats.

Porpoises are often confused with dolphins. Here are a couple examples of their differences. The fin on the back of a porpoise is shaped more like a triangle, and their faces are rounded, where a dolphin has a long "beak" and a more curved fin on its back.

DOLPHIN

PORPOISE

What are SEA SPARKLES?

Sea sparkles are tiny single-celled organisms called dinoflagellates.

Most dinoflagellates live in the ocean, but some live in fresh water.

Only a few dinoflagellates can make glow-in-the-dark light.

FEELINGS

David B had many emotions in this story.

Do you remember when he was happy, scared, or surprised?

Were there other emotions he had?

What makes you happy?

Have you been scared or surprised?

WORDS to KNOW

ANCHOR

SEA

TREES

TWILIGHT

CHANNEL

PROPELLER

DINOFLAGELLATES

PORPOISE

STEW

MOON

WORDS SEARCH

1. The wise old __ __ __ __ __ that live along the shore make up a large area of land called a forest.

2. A __ __ __ is a large body of saltwater that is part of an ocean.

3. What kind of animal is David B's friend, Dolly? __ __ __ __ __ __ __ __.

4. Sea sparkles are teeny-tiny creatures called __ __ __ __ __ __ __ __ __ __ __ __ __ __.

5. When David B was scared in the dark, he was afraid the rocks were going to make him into __ __ __ __.

6. David B wished he was home in Comfy Cove with this heavy object keeping him securely in place. What is that object? __ __ __ __ __ __

7. The time of day when the sea sparkles began to fade is known as __ __ __ __ __ __ __ __. It's the time when the light in the sky is changing between day and night or night and day.

8. David B's friend the __ __ __ __ was high in the night sky when he decided to stay up all night.

9. The type of waterway that David B loves to cruise is called a __ __ __ __ __ __ __. It's a passage or strait between two land masses.

10. The part of David B that spins and makes him go is the __ __ __ __ __ __ __ __ __.

CPSIA information can be obtained at www.ICGtesting.com
Printed in the USA
BVIW121947210319
543259BV00001B/3